The Very First
Christmas

Edited by Anna Milbourne
Adapted from *The First Christmas*,
written by Heather Amery and designed by Laura Fearn

The Very First
Christmas

Louie Stowell
Illustrated by Elena Temporin

Designed by Nelupa Hussain

Once, in a town called Nazareth,
there lived a girl named Mary.

One day an angel flew down
to her from heaven.

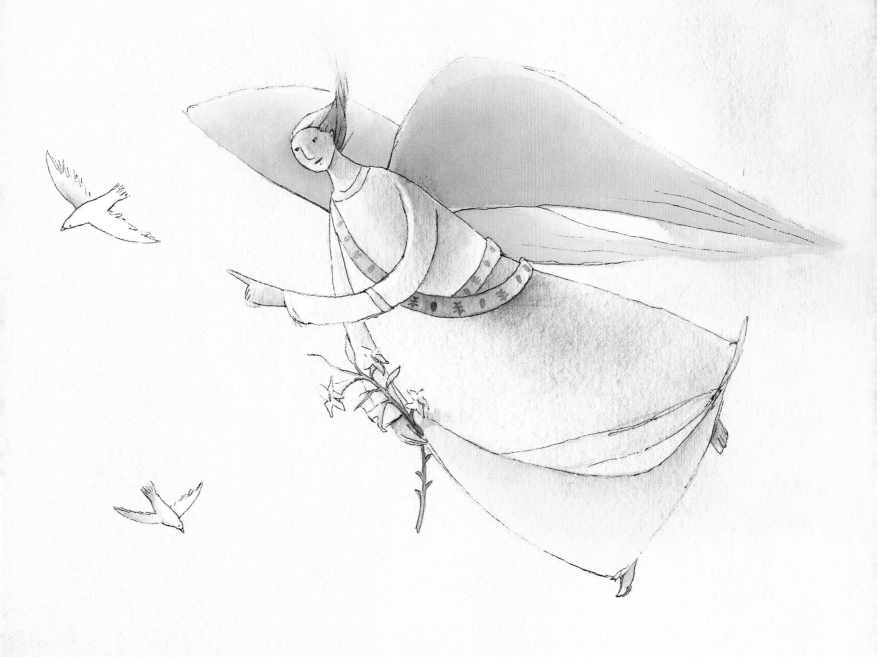

"I have good news," the angel said.
    "God has chosen you to have his baby son."

The months flew by and Mary
married a carpenter named Joseph.
It was almost time for the baby to be born.

Then a message came from the rulers
of the land. Everybody had to go
to their family's home town to be counted.

"My family came from Bethlehem," said Joseph.
"That's where we will have to go."

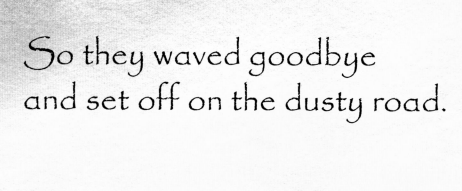

So they waved goodbye
and set off on the dusty road.

Mary rode on a little donkey
and Joseph walked by her side...

...all the way to Bethlehem.

When they arrived, it was nearly dark.
Joseph knock-knock-knocked
at the door of an inn.

"I'm sorry," said the innkeeper,
"but we don't have any room."

So Joseph knocked at another door,
and another and another.

But no one had any room for them.

When the very last innkeeper shook
his head, they didn't know what to do.

Then the innkeeper had an idea.
"I have a stable that's warm and dry.
You could sleep there tonight."

Later that night,
Mary gave birth to a baby boy.

"Your name is Jesus," she whispered.

Out on the hills,
shepherds were watching their sheep.

Suddenly, an angel appeared in the sky.
His voice rang out like a thousand bells...

"Tonight, the son of God was born in a stable in Bethlehem."

The shepherds couldn't wait to visit the baby.

They rushed to the stable and peeked inside.
"Come in," said Mary gently.

So they gathered around the manger
where the tiny baby lay.

Far away in the East,
three wise men saw a star.

"It's a sign that the son of God
has been born," said one of them.

They followed the star across the desert
until they got to Bethlehem.

The star shone down
on the little stable.
Could this really be the place?

The wise men came in quietly
and knelt before the manger.

They offered baby Jesus gifts
of gold, frankincense and myrrh.

That was the very first Christmas...

...and it was a very happy Christmas indeed.